Pam's Maps

Pippa Goodhart

Katherine Lodge

Jolly Washtub

Red Fox

Jolly Washtub

Little Jolly Washtub

For a long time, all that the crew of the
Jolly Washtub had seen was sea. But one
day little Pam shouted out, "Land ahoy!"
"Hooray!" cheered the pirates.

"Arr," said Captain Scarnose.
"There it be at last – the island
where I buried my treasure
all them long years ago.
Now we'll be rich!"

"Are you sure it's the same
island?" asked Pam.

6

"Has it got a sandy beach and trees?" asked the captain.

Pam looked through her telescope. "Yes," she said.

"Then that's the island we're after," said the captain.

But don't lots of islands have sand and trees?

Of CAWS they do.

Well I just hope it's the right one!

They anchored the *Jolly Washtub* near the island and got ready to land.

8

"Where is the treasure on the island?" asked Chewear.

"Don't you worry your ugly little head about that," said the captain.

"You just follow me."

Who are they?

So they landed on the sand.

Hey, look at me.

10

Captain Scarnose uncurled a piece of paper.
"What's that?" asked Pam.
"Arr," said Captain Scarnose. "I ain't stupid, you know. This be my list of instructions. They tell how to find the place where X marks the spot. That's where I buried the treasure. Follow me, shipmates!"

Where the Treasure Be Hid and How to Find It.

1 Land on the land.
2 Follow the footprints over the sand.
3 Turn right and take sixty steps.
4 See where the sun sits in the sky. Take one step towards the sun, then dig.

X Marks the spot.

They had already done number one on the list of instructions.

"See?" said the captain. "It's easy. All we've got to do now is follow number two: 'Follow the footprints over the sand'."

"Which footprints?" asked Knottytail. "There are footprints going off all over the place."

"Oh, lor," said Captain Scarnose. "That ain't right at all. It was the footprints I left after I buried the treasure that we need. Those are the footprints that'll lead us back to the treasure."

"But those footprints must have been washed off the sand ages ago," said Pam.

"What? You mean they're gone?" said the captain.

"Completely gone," said Pam.

"Oh, lor! Whatever am I to do?"

"Go on to number three," said Pam.

"'Turn right and take sixty steps'."

No, these footprints.

"Right, boys," said the captain.

"We have to turn right."

So they all did.

"Whose right?" asked Chewear.

"That's right!"

"No, you're wrong. That is right!"

"I'm right, of course." Captain Scarnose was getting cross. "The captain is always right. Didn't you know that? So follow me and count!"

They all followed Captain Scarnose.
"This ain't going to work," said Chewear.
"We ain't never going to be rich. I'll be eating
seaweed porridge for the rest of my days."

...4, 5, 6, 7, 8, 9, 10...

"I've done seventy steps already," said Pam. "Of *caws* you have! That's because you've got the littlest legs and have to take more steps to cover the same ground," said Crow.

...25, 26, 27, 28, 29, 30...

...35, 36...

"Almost there, boys. I reckon I can smell treasure in the air!" said Captain Scarnose. "Instruction number four: 'See where the sun sits in the sky. Take one step towards the sun, then dig. X marks the spot.' Where's the sun, boys?"

"In the sky, Captain."

"I know that, jellyfish brain!" said the captain.

"But which part of the sky, eh?"
Knottytail pointed.

21

Where is it?

"That's it, then," said the captain, and he took a step towards the sun. "Dig just here!"

"Where's the famous X then?" asked Chewear.

"Isn't the sun in different parts of the sky at different times of day?" asked Pam.

"Of *caws* it is! He's got it all wrong!" said Crow.

"Get digging!" said the captain.

They dug and dug and the sun began to go down. "There's nothing there, Captain!" said Chewear.

"There must be! Keep digging!" said Captain Scarnose.

"How come you never do any digging, Captain?" asked Knottytail.

"Because I'm busy thinking. Without me, you'd all be lost. Keep digging, boys!"

"Well, I'm not a boy so shall we go exploring, Crow?" said Pam.

"But . . . !" began the captain, but Pam and Crow had gone.

Pam and Crow flew high into the sky.

"Oh, look," said Pam, "there's the X marking the spot! I can see the treasure place and our ship and everything!"

"Of *caws* you can!" said Crow.

"But how will I remember the way to the treasure when I get down on the ground again?" asked Pam. "The captain's way didn't work. I'll have to think of something better."

On the beach, Pam began to draw in the sand.

"What be that?" asked Captain Scarnose.

"A picture to show where your treasure is," said Pam. "I've seen the X marking the spot!"

"Have you, by barnacles? Right then, boys!" said the captain. "Let's go!"

But the sun had almost set. "Tell you what, Captain," said Pam, "you make the supper. Then I'll make a picture that you can carry with you tomorrow to show you the way to the treasure."

"Me, make supper?" said Captain Scarnose. "Captains don't cook!"

"Do you want a map or not?" asked Pam.

"Oh, yes, er, righto," said the captain. "Fetch the potato peeler and sling those hammocks, boys!"

Mmm.

yum yum.

Give us a break Captain.

THE Pirate Cook Book

The pirates slept and snored, all of them except for Pam.

cave great for

forest

sea

my favourite tree

this way t

hole
pirat
d

where we
have walked

our
sandcastles

funny shaped roc

beach

She worked by moonlight to make her map.

Next morning, the pirates were woken by boats of visitors arriving.

34

"This be the day that we make our fortunes, boys!" said Captain Scarnose. "Quick, before these others get it. Follow me!"

Even Captain Scarnose found it easy to follow Pam's map.

"Look for the tall tree on top of the hill, boys!" he said. "Then follow that path there to the rock . . ."

Get digging!

"... Yo, ho ho, I see my X at last! Have you got your shovels shark-sharp and ready, boys? Get digging!"

While the boys dug and dug and dug and found a tiny bit of treasure ...

. . . Pam was busy on the beach.
She made maps for all the visitors
and sold them.

"There's a lovely place
to swim," Pam told the visitors.
Crow gave them
rides in the sky.

39

Pam and Crow made lots of money.

The captain and his pirates made lots of mess.

Got it at last! Let's show it to Pam.

They met Pam at the beach.

"Well, dang me!" said Captain Scarnose. "I reckon it's little Pam who's the one with the brains around here!"

"How ever did you get that treasure without digging?" asked Chewear.

"I did work and got paid for it," said Pam.

"Couldn't we try that too?" asked Knottytail.

"Would you like to sell ice creams?" asked Pam.

"Ooo, yes please!" said Knottytail.

Ice cream 20p

Climb the sand sculpture 20p

Chewear made a sand sculpture. And Captain Scarnose buried treasure. The visitors bought Pam's maps to help them find it. So everyone was happy.

Weasel has made a map of the park. A map is a picture of a place that shows where things are. He has hidden some treasure for his friends to find. Can you see it? Here's how you can play, too!

YOU WILL NEED: paper, a pen, treasure to hide (an apple, a picture, a sweet)

1. Go to the park with an adult and look around to see where everything is. Make a list of all the things that you want to show on your map.

2. Decide what symbols to use for each of the things on your list. Here are some examples of symbols for things you might find in the park:

Symbols are simple pictures. They help people to understand what you have drawn.

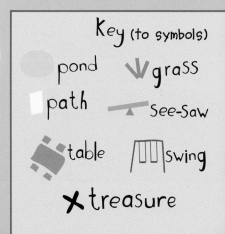

Key (to symbols)

pond   W grass

path   see-saw

table   swing

✗ treasure

3. Next, draw the shape of the park. Then draw on the gates, paths and fences.

4. Add your symbols for the big things in the park, like the pond.

5. Draw in your symbols for the other things on your list.

6. Hide your treasure. Mark where it is hidden with an X. Now give the map to your friends. How fast can they find the treasure?

You can hunt for treasure in your bedroom or garden, too!

Proper maps don't measure distance with footprints. They use units such as metres.

Pippa Goodhart

Where did you get the idea for this story? I thought of this story when I was climbing a mountain. I looked down on a valley from high up and it looked like a map. I decided to call the main character Pam because her name spells 'map' backwards!

What do you do if you get stuck on a story? If I get stuck, I leave the story and do something else. A nice hot bubbly bath is my best place for thinking through story problems.

Have you ever hunted for buried treasure? The only treasure I've ever found are odd coins on the pavement or down the side of sofa cushions.

Have you ever made a map of your own? I've made little maps of roads to show people how to find my house.

Are you good at reading maps? No! My husband tried to teach me how to read a map and use a compass and I went in exactly the wrong direction!

Did you always want to be a writer? No. I used to want to be a fireman. But being a writer is lovely.